A book to assist adults in helping children unpack, understand, and manage their feelings and emotions

# Talking ABOUT FeeLiNGS

by Jayneen Sanders    illustrated by Cherie Zamazing

For Sophie

Because we miss you
and we love you.

J.S.

Talking About Feelings
Educate2Empower Publishing an imprint of
UpLoad Publishing Pty Ltd
Victoria Australia
www.upload.com.au

First published in 2018

Written by Jayneen Sanders
Illustrations by Cherie Zamazing

Jayneen Sanders asserts her right to be identified as the author of this work.
Cherie Zamazing asserts her right to be identified as the illustrator of this work.

Designed by Stephanie Spartels, Studio Spartels

ISBN: 9781925089301 (hbk) 9781925089073 (pbk)

A catalogue record for this
book is available from the
National Library of Australia

Disclaimer: The information in this book is advice only written by the author based on her advocacy in this area, and her experience working with children as a classroom teacher and mother. The information is not meant to be a substitute for professional advice. If you are concerned about a child's behavior seek professional help.

# Note to the Reader

The aim of this book is to assist adults in helping children unpack, understand and manage their feelings and emotions in an engaging and interactive way. Children, particularly young children, do not have the vocabulary or the experience to draw upon to express exactly how they are feeling. It is important for children to understand that feelings fluctuate and to never judge themselves negatively for experiencing challenging emotions. Similarly, adults should be accepting of a child's feelings — no matter how challenging or insignificant they may seem. A child should never be made to feel that their emotions are wrong or shameful. This only leads to negative self-talk. This book has been designed to assist parents, caregivers, educators and health professionals to help children understand what they are feeling and why they might feel that way, and to encourage them to talk about and describe their feelings and emotions in a non-pressured, guided and safe environment. The questions in this book are suggestions only. The adult who is using this book with the child needs to follow the child's lead in order to have a meaningful and authentic discussion. **I strongly suggest using this book over a number of sessions, working through it slowly and at the child's pace; ensuring they have sufficient time to respond. This book should be thought of as a series of stimuli designed to initiate discussions about the child's feelings. It is NOT a series of questions that must be answered in a linear way. Be prepared to stop and listen to the child and be flexible in the use of this book.**

It is also important that the adult is an active listener, i.e. taking the time to 'hear' what the child may be trying to convey. This book can be used by an adult who may have specific concerns about a child, or who simply wishes to 'check in' to see how a child is fairing. Talking about challenging emotions and accumulating a ready bank of 'feeling' words helps a child to better express their emotions rather than act them out through negative behaviors. **Before using this book with a child, please familiarize yourself with the entire contents and read 'Using this Book' on pages 34-37 so you are familiar with the questions and format.**

# Why It Is Important for Children to Talk About Their Feelings

Expanding emotional awareness in children will nurture the development of their emotional intelligence. This in turn will build their capacity to relate to the world and the people in it with sensitivity, courage and honesty. Emotional intelligence fuels healthy friendships, leads to better decision-making, increases the capacity for children to express themselves and have their needs met positively, and contributes to academic success. When it comes to our children, we can't choose their temperament and we can't choose their personality, but we can shape it. As the important adults in their lives, we have enormous capacity to fuel their flight. Expanding their emotional awareness is a powerful way to do this.

BY KAREN YOUNG
psychologist, author  www.heysigmund.com

Everyone has **feelings**.

You have feelings and your friends have feelings.

The big people around you have feelings too.

You might feel **happy** in the morning because you can play outside.

But you might feel **sad** in the afternoon because you can't.

A feeling might last for a long time or it might last for a short time.

Our feelings are always changing.

Look at this child.

This child's feelings are always changing too!

happy

worried

brave

Scared

angry

lonely/sad

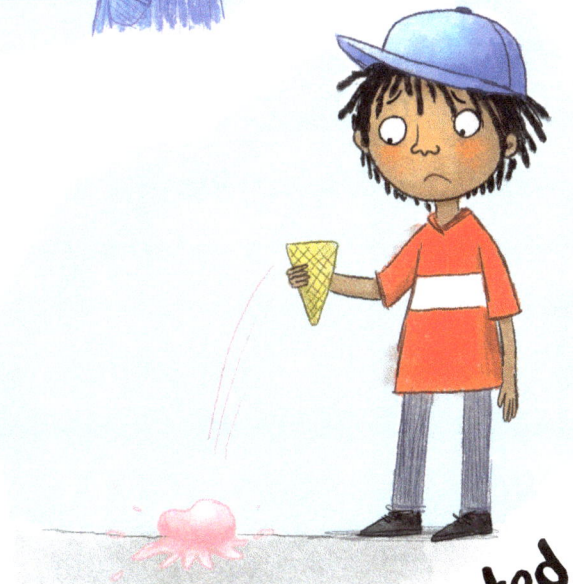

disappointed

9

**Sometimes you might feel really happy.**

What color do you think happy might be?

Why is ----------------- happy for you?

**Sometimes you might feel sad.**

What color do you think sad might be?

Why is ----------------- sad for you?

**And sometimes you might feel angry.**

What color do you think angry might be?

Why is ----------------- angry for you?

What color do you think ----------------- might be?

Why is ----------------------------------- for you?

Some feelings are so BIG, we just don't know what to do!

We might feel ...

**sad**

or **worried**

or **angry**

or **scared**.

When we have those feelings, we need to talk to an adult who makes us feel safe and who we trust.

That person will help us to understand those BIG feelings.

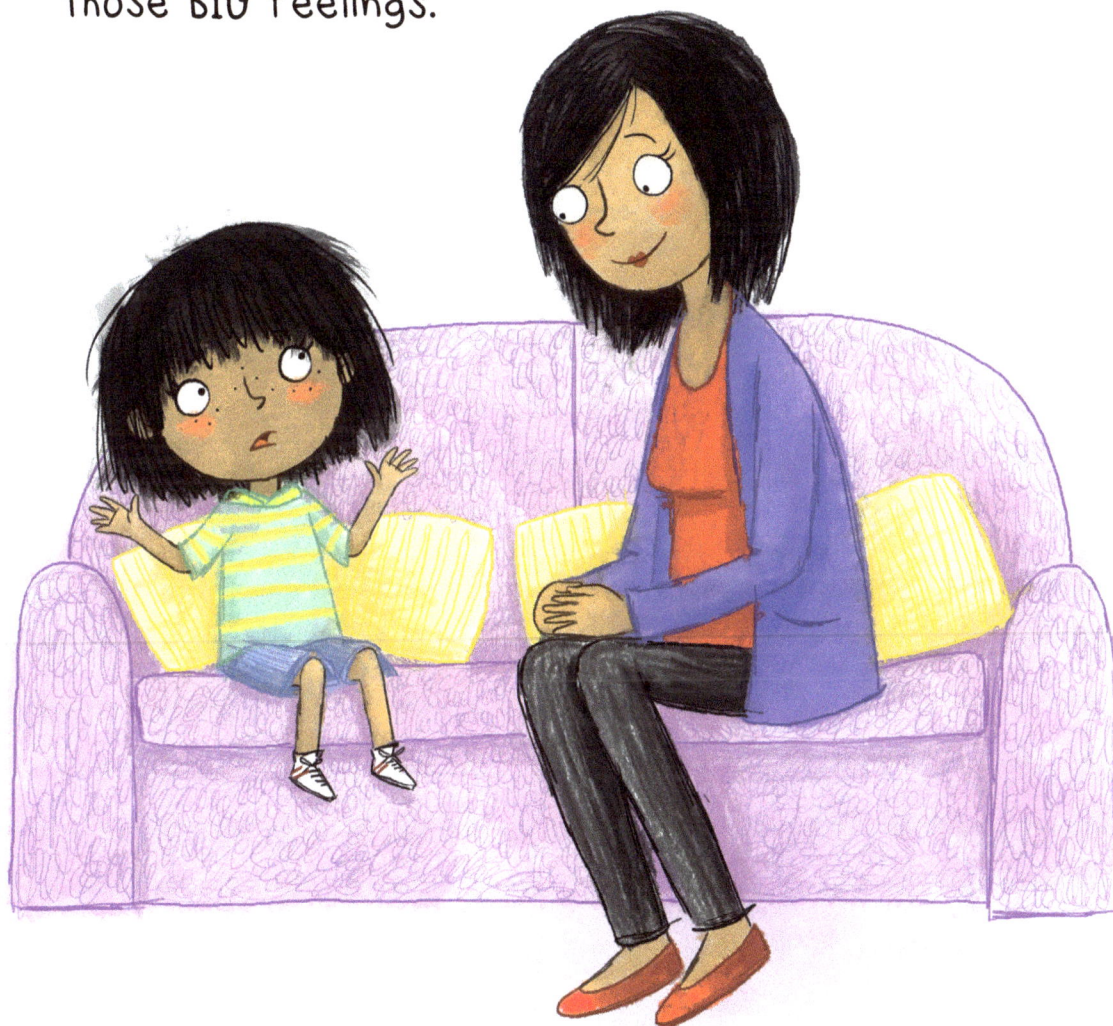

Who could you tell your BIG feelings to?

Let's talk about **your** feelings.

There will be some questions for you to think about.

You can stop and talk to the person reading
with you at any time.

Are you ready? Let's go!

What color is your feeling today?

Where do you feel this
color in your body?

How BIG is your feeling today?

Does it feel as BIG as a mountain?

Or as small as a button?

Or does it feel middle-sized ...
like the size of a chair?

If you could touch your feeling, how might it feel?

**spikey**

**prickly**

**wibbly wobbly**

**bumpy**

**flat**

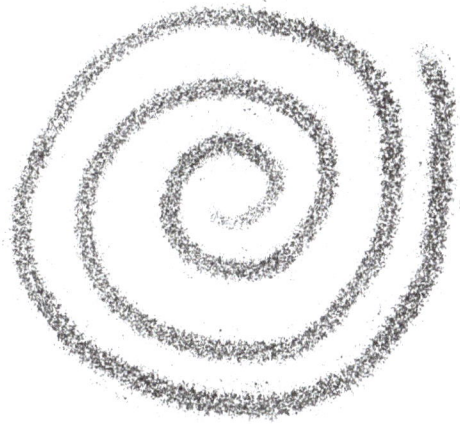

**swirly**

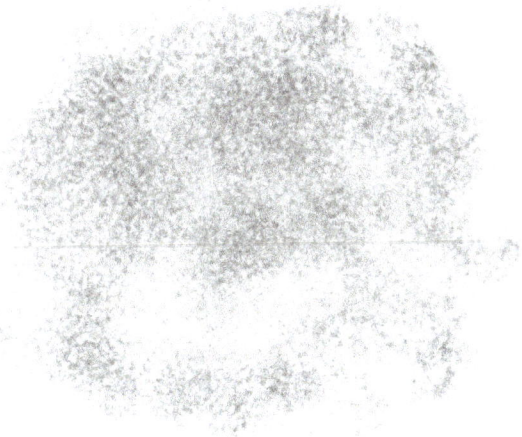

**soft**

**hard**

Maybe it doesn't feel like any of these things . . .

If you could draw your feeling, what would it look like?

Would you like to draw your feeling?

Talking about a feeling can be really helpful too.

Would you like to use your own words to talk about your feeling?

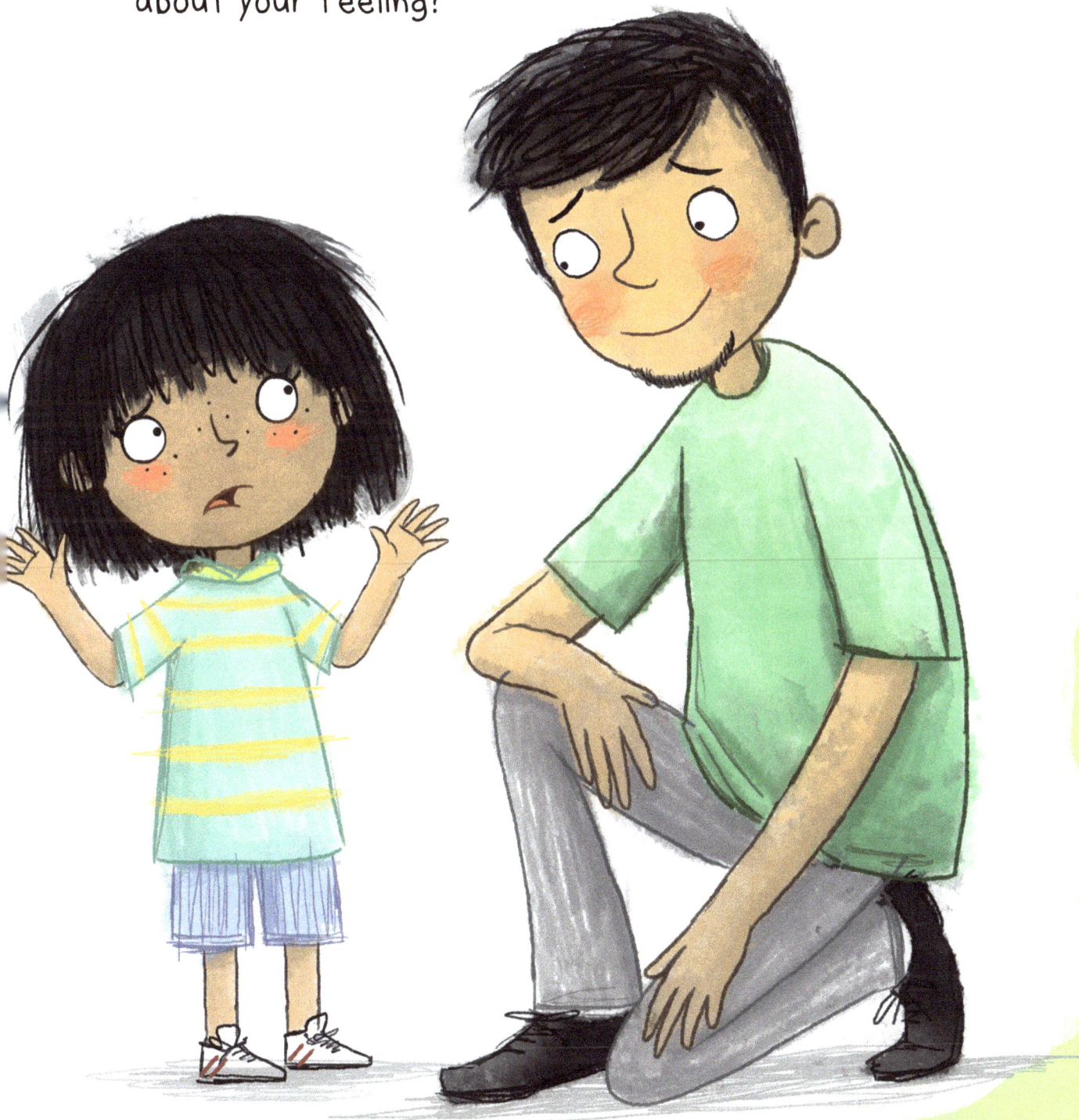

Feelings often come from ...

- something we are doing or thinking about

- something that is happening around us or something that has happened to us

- or from other people.

But sometimes we don't know where our feelings come from.

Do you know where your feeling has come from today?

Look at this child.*

How do you think the child is feeling in this picture?

Now **you** choose one of the faces. How do you think the child is feeling in this picture? Why might the child be feeling this way?

Choose another face. How do you think the child is feeling in this picture?

Do you ever feel like this?

When might you feel like this?

(* Reader points to a face.)

The big person who is reading this book with you can talk about their feelings too.

Why don't you ask them how they are feeling today?

Ask them why they are feeling that way.

A book to assist adults in helping children unpack, understand, and manage their feelings and emotions

Talking ABOUT FeeLiNGS

by Jayneen Sanders    illustrated by Cherie Zamazing

Do you ever feel angry like this child?

When do you feel angry?

What could you do if you feel angry?

Do you ever feel sad? When do you feel sad?

What could you do if you feel sad?

Do you ever feel worried or scared? When do you feel worried or scared? What could you do if you feel this way?

Do you ever feel _____ ?

When do you feel _____ ?

What could you do if you feel _____ ?

What makes you feel happy?

What color do you think happy might be?

Where might you feel happy in your body?

How big do you think happy is?

What might happy feel like to touch?

Happy sounds like fun.

You have been so awesome talking about your feelings today.

Give yourself a big warm hug. You are amazing!

Are you feeling proud? I am proud of you too!

# USING THIS BOOK

The following ideas and questions are a guide only. In order to have an authentic discussion between the child and yourself, try to follow their lead. Encourage them to keep talking if they wish to discuss a particular aspect or section of the book. Also don't be afraid to ask your own questions, if they seem appropriate, regarding the direction the child is taking the discussion. This book is by no means rigid in its format. It has been designed to be flexible to suit the needs of the child and their own unique experiences. If there is silence after a question, allow the child time and space to say how they are really feeling. Try to avoid leading them; otherwise, there is a possibility they may answer in a way they believe you want them to respond.

*Note: as a child's vocabulary increases, encourage them to use a bank of feeling words to express their emotions beyond 'sad' or 'happy' such as surprised, brave, joyful, worried, angry, frightened, bored, proud, shy, embarrassed, friendly, calm, quiet, curious, confused, safe, unsafe, relieved, jealous, frustrated, excited, uncomfortable, silly, forgotten, ignored, loved, curious, interested, engaged, overwhelmed, terrified and peaceful.*

Ultimately, this book and the discussions it generates will give children the confidence to understand and express their feelings in their own unique way.

## Options for use

1. Read and discuss the complete book with the child over one session. This option can only work if the child is allowed to break when required and there is no sense of pressure.

2. Read and discuss the complete book with the child over a number of sessions, i.e. break the discussion when a pause organically develops.

3. Revisit pages 16 to 25 with the child (the explanation on page 24 could be left out) if the complete book has been read at another time. This might be because you are worried about a child, and you are trying to find out what is troubling them. *Note: these pages have a green border.*

4. Use pages 16 to 21 as a simple conversation starter with the child, i.e. 'checking in' with them to see if they are doing 'okay'.

*Note: the central character's name is Boo and she/he is intended to be gender-neutral. However, you may suggest to the child you are using this book with to provide this character with any name they wish.*

## Pages 4-5

Point to particular children in the picture and ask how they might be feeling and why they might be feeling that way. Discuss some of the adults in the picture and ask who they might be in relation to the children. Talk about how the adults may be feeling. Ask, 'Who are the big people in your life who are very important to you?'

## Pages 6-7

Ask, 'Do you like to play outside/inside? Why do you think our feelings are always changing?'

## Pages 8-9

The central aim of this page is for children to realize that our feelings and emotions are always changing. Say, 'Look at this child. How is he feeling in this picture? What about this picture? Notice how his feelings are always changing.' Relate the idea of our changing feelings back to the child and ask, 'How did you feel at bedtime last night? Do you feel the same today?' Connect with some of your own examples such as, 'I felt worried this morning because I thought I would miss my bus but now I feel happy because I'm talking with you!' If you wish to open up the discussion further, another option could be to ask, 'How is the child feeling in this picture? How might you feel in this situation?' Connect with a child on a more personal level by offering your own experiences to help open up a dialogue, e.g. 'The first time I went on a slide, I was so scared that it took a long time before I was brave enough to go down. When I was your age, my friend's dog jumped up on me and it didn't make me happy, it made me scared.' Point out that different scenarios elicit different feelings and emotions from individual people, i.e. what makes one person happy (a dog licking them) may make another person scared. You could also go further and talk about the

fact that we can feel two emotions at one time, e.g. we may feel disappointed that our ice-cream scoop fell to the ground but we might feel angry also. It is important that children realize their feelings are always changing (and that's okay) and that people can react differently to the same situation.

## Pages 10-11

The purpose of this page is to act as a 'key' to the child's feelings and emotions. The color a child chooses to associate with an emotion may prove interesting; it may not always be what you expect. For example, a young boy told me the color he associated with being scared was yellow because it is the color of sparks in an explosion. You may wish to ask the child about 'happy', 'sad' or 'angry' or you may wish to only ask about 'happy' and then go straight to the blank questions in order to specifically target a certain feeling with the child. These pages are meant to be flexible, but they will give you an insight into the colors a child associates with a feeling in this particular session. *Note: with some children a color or colors might change in different sessions. Also some children may choose more than one color and associate them with a particular feeling, and that is absolutely okay.*

## Pages 12-13

Discuss the faces and the matching emotions featured on the character on this page. Guide the discussion around to who the child trusts and who they feel safe telling their 'big' feelings to. A child might name one adult or a number of adults. Once again, be lead by the child.

## Pages 14-15

As per the page.

## Pages 16-17

Read the first question to the child. Give them time to think about their answer. They may point to a color/s or name the color/s. From pages 10—11 you will have an idea of what color a child associates with what feeling/s. Then ask, 'Where do you feel this color in your body?' This question allows the child to focus on a part of their body they associate with the emotion/s, e.g. a child might select the color gray (sadness for them) and point to their throat (where the tears have become stuck).

## Pages 18-19

The images on these pages are purposely chosen so the child does not have a strong connection to them, e.g. if a cat had been drawn to illustrate 'middle-sized', the child may have chosen 'middle—sized' to describe their feeling simply because they like cats rather than how big the feeling actually feels. Some emotions can feel enormous for a child and being able to articulate a size is another tool to help them unpack what they are feeling.

## Pages 20-21

These pages provide the child with a vehicle to identify what a feeling might be like if they could touch it. If the feeling doesn't feel like any of these images, you could ask the child to find something in the room that their feeling may 'feel like' to touch.

## Pages 22-23

Provide the opportunity for the child to draw their feeling if it is something the child would like to do. Provide colored pencils (in the colors on pages 10—11) and paper for the child and take note of the colors they use in their drawing. You could ask the child to tell you about their picture. Some children appreciate the opportunity to talk about their feeling/s based around what they have drawn. Again, this should be child lead and the choice theirs.

## Pages 24-25

Read each point slowly to the child, so they can think about each statement and absorb the meaning as it relates to their situation.

*Point 1: Ask, 'What is something you could be doing that makes you feel happy/scared, etc.?' Talk to the child about a certain way of thinking and how the way we think about a situation actually changes our feelings, e.g. ask the child to imagine meeting a dog at the park — say, 'If you think ... "cute dog" then you will feel happy about the meeting; but if you think the dog might bite you, then you will feel scared, worried and anxious about the situation. The way we think about a situation greatly affects our feelings.'*

*Point 2: Discuss how sometimes things happening around us make us feel a certain way, e.g. fireworks might make one person feel excited, while another person may feel anxious. Explain that sometimes things might happen to us, e.g. we leave our teddy on the train and because of that happening to us we feel sad.*

*Point 3: Ask, 'Does another person/s make you feel happy/scared/angry, etc.?' Talk about how other people's emotions and/or actions can make us feel a certain way, e.g. a person may push us and make us feel scared. Explain that sometimes we feel a certain way and we really don't know why, and that's okay.*

Ask, 'Do you know where your feeling has come from today?' and allow the child time to talk about this. This question is an important conversation starter.

## Pages 26-27

Read through the questions with the child. I suggest when you choose a face, choose an emotion you know the child is not experiencing currently. This is so when they get to choose, they have the option of choosing the emotion they are experiencing currently. Let the discussion around the second and third faces organically develop and be child lead. However, if the child has not selected the emotion you believe they may be experiencing, and you wish to explore it further, you could choose a face/feeling to unpack. On pages 38—39 you will find the 'Key to Faces'. These labels are for your reference only. When a child is talking about an emotion on pages 26—27, allow them to interpret the faces as they wish, i.e. a face that portrays 'guilty' to you may in fact portray 'scared' to a child. The 'Key to Faces' page is a guide for the adult only. *Note: here is a game you could play at any time (just open up at this page). Have the child close their eyes and randomly point to a face. Now have them open their eyes and ask them what they think that feeling might be. Encourage them to talk about a time when they experienced that feeling. If they find it difficult to talk about the feeling, they could draw a picture representing the time/s they felt that way.*

## Pages 28-29

It is important for children to understand that adults have feelings and emotions too, and that they can talk about them. Model this by talking about your own feelings in an open and honest way.

## Pages 30-31

These two pages are quite intense and may take some time to explore with the child. You may like to go through all three scenarios if time permits, or two or one or none; or you may only explore the questions you know will benefit the child the most, e.g. 'Do you ever feel *lonely*?' (As you know the child has few friends or may be being bullied.) 'When do you feel *lonely*? What could you do if you feel *lonely*?' Ensure you have strategies to assist the child when you come to the third question.

## SUGGESTED STRATEGIES

### *What could you do if you feel angry?*

- Have the child focus on taking a deep breath followed by a slow release. Using a bubble blower is an ideal way to practice this.

- Have the child think of their favorite food that is eaten hot, and imagine they can smell it. Ask them to take a deep breath in and then slowly blow out as if they were cooling the food.

### *What could you do if you feel sad?*

- Ask the child to wrap their arms around their body and give themself a big hug. Then they could tell you how 'sad' makes them feel.

- Suggest the child reads their favorite book or watches their favorite TV show snuggled up with their favorite toy or blanket.

### *What could you do if you feel worried or scared?*

- Talk with the child about the situation of why they are anxious, e.g. going to a class swimming lesson. Go over where it will be, how they will get there, what will happen once they arrive. They could even role-play the bus ride and what they will do once they are at the venue.

- See the children's book *How Big Are Your Worries Little Bear?* for more ideas on how to help children with anxiety. Available at www.e2epublishing.info

### *What could you do if you feel lonely?*

- Suggest to the child that they talk to someone who makes them feel safe about how they are feeling.

- If the child is lonely at school, suggest they take some paper and pencils with them and draw or write stories in a safe space at school. The teacher could encourage others to join them.

## Pages 32-33

End the session on a 'happy' and positive note and discuss what it's like to feel happy. Giving themselves a hug is something all kids can do and is comforting. If appropriate, you could ask the child if they want a hug from you, and if they consent, then a hug is always nice! Ensure the child knows they have done a great job and that you are proud of them. A great outcome for the session is that the child also feels proud of themself and this has been internalized.

# Key to Faces on Pages 26-27

worried

proud

calm

happy

sad

brave

angry

scared

disappointed

confused

lonely

shame

guilty

embarrassed

excited

# Books by the Same Author

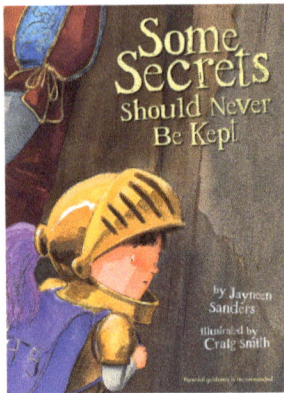

### Some Secrets Should Never Be Kept

This book sensitively broaches the subject of safe and unsafe touch, and assists caregivers and educators to broach this subject with children in a non-threatening and age-appropriate way. Discussion Questions included. Ages 3 to 11 years.

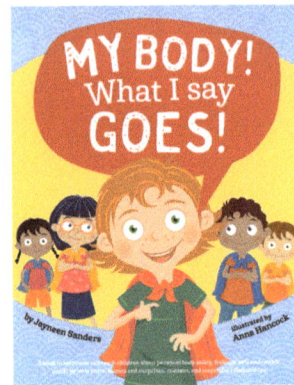

### My Body! What I Say Goes!

A children's picture book to empower and teach children about personal body safety, feelings, safe and unsafe touch, private parts, secrets and surprises, consent and respect. Discussion Questions included. Ages 3 to 9 years.

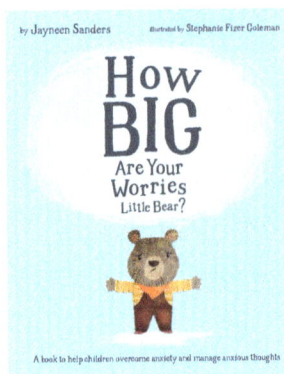

### How Big Are Your Worries Little Bear?

This book was written to help children overcome fears and anxious thoughts by providing them with life-long skills in how to deal with anxiety. Discussion Questions and hints to help anxious children included. Ages 3 to 9 years.

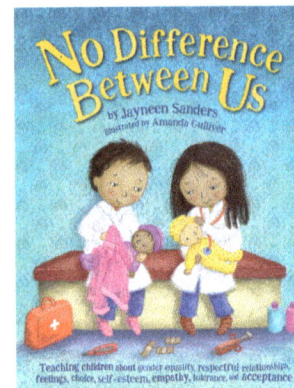

### No Difference Between Us

Jess is a girl and Ben is a boy but in all the BIG ways there is no difference between them. A story to explore gender equality, respectful relationships, feelings and self-esteem. Discussion Questions included. Ages 2 to 9 years.

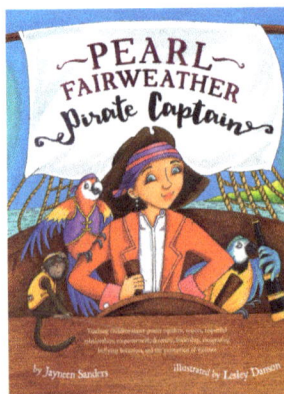

### Pearl Fairweather, Pirate Captain

Through an engaging narrative, this beautifully illustrated children's book explores gender equality, respect, diversity, leadership, and recognizing bullying behaviors. Discussion Questions included. Ages 5 to 12 years.

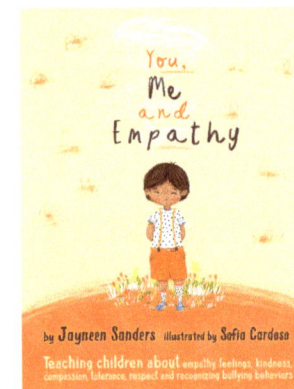

### You, Me and Empathy

This charming story uses verse, beautiful illustrations and a little person called Quinn to model the meaning of empathy, kindness and compassion. Discussion Questions and activities to promote empathy and kindness included. Ages 3 to 9 years.

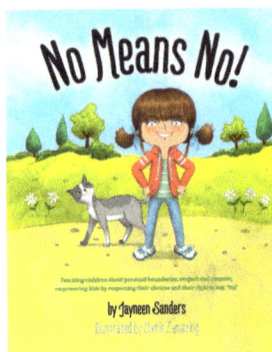

### No Means No!

A story about an empowered little girl with a strong voice on all issues, especially those relating to her body! A book to teach children about personal body boundaries, respect and consent. Discussion Questions included. Ages 2 to 9 years.

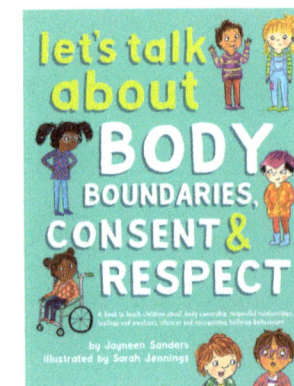

### Let's Talk About Body Boundaries, Consent and Respect

Through familiar scenarios, this book opens up crucial conversations with children around consent and respect. Discussion Questions included. Ages 4 to 10 years.

For more information go to: www.e2epublishing.info